All of the

by Liza Charlesworth

ISBN: 978-1-338-78275-2
Illustrated by Kevin Zimmer
Copyright © 2021 by Liza Charlesworth. All rights reserved.
Published by Scholastic Inc., 557 Broadway, New York, NY 10012
10 9 8 7 6 5 4 3 2 1   68   21 22 23 24 25 26 27/0
Printed in Jiaxing, China. First printing, June 2021.

All of the bats went to the garden.
Flap, flap!

BAT GARDEN

All of the bats went to the lake. Flap, flap!

3

All of the bats went to the park. Flap, flap!

BAT PARK

4

All of the bats went to the beach. Flap, flap!

5

All of the bats went to the mountain. Flap, flap!

BAT MOUNTAIN

6

All of the bats went to the cave. Flap, flap!

BAT CAVE

All of the bats
went to sleep.
Nap, nap!